Curious George®
Colors Eggs

Adaptation by Kate O'Sullivan
Based on the TV series teleplay
written by Michael Maurer

Houghton Mifflin Harcourt Publishing Company
Boston New York 2011

For information about permission to reproduce selections from this book, write to Permissions, Houghton Mifflin Harcourt Publishing Company, 215 Park Avenue South, New York, New York 10003.

Library of Congress Cataloging-in-Publication Data is on file.

ISBN: 978-0-547-55904-9 paper-over-board
ISBN: 978-0-547-31585-0 paperback

Design by Afsoon Razavi

www.hmhbooks.com

Printed in China
LEO 10 9 8 7 6 5 4 3 2 1
4500317939

AGES	GRADES	GUIDED READING LEVEL	READING RECOVERY LEVEL	LEXILE ® LEVE
5-7	1-2	I	15-16	330L

George was excited.
He was spending the day with
Betsy and Steve.

They were going to dye eggs!
There would be an egg hunt later.
The man with the yellow hat gave
George an apron.
"I am leaving for my bird-watching
trip with Chef Pisghetti. Please try to
stay clean while I am gone," he said.

Steve showed George three pots of dye.
One was red. One was blue. And one
was yellow.
"These are called primary colors,"
Steve said.
"You can make every color in the
rainbow. Just mix them in different
ways."

George was very curious.

Steve dipped an egg in the yellow dye.

Then Steve
dipped the egg
in the blue dye.
The egg turned green!

George had an idea.

He dipped a
banana in blue dye.
Then he dipped it in the red dye.
George made the banana turn
purple!

Charkie was curious, too.
She wanted to see the purple
banana up close.

She chased after George.
As they ran, Charkie bumped the
tables. One started to roll.

It knocked down a mop.
The mop bumped a shelf.
And the cake on the shelf started to fall!

George jumped, losing his apron.
He saved the cake!
But it was very heavy.
His feet started to slip . . .

"Oh, no, George!" Steve cried.
He and Betsy grabbed the cake.
But George fell into the pot! "You were
supposed to stay clean," said Betsy.

But George had another idea.
If red and blue made purple,
could he mix the right colors to make
brown?

George jumped into the red dye.
But yellow and red made orange,
not brown.

George and his
friends heard footsteps in the hall.
"Quick—hide!" Steve said.
George jumped into the sink.

"How was the egg dyeing?" the
man with the yellow hat asked.
"And where's George?" asked
Chef Pisghetti.

George popped up from the sink.
"Thanks for staying clean," said his
friend. George had picked the perfect
hiding place.

Colors, Colors, Everywhere!

Circle all of the objects in primary colors (red, yellow, blue).